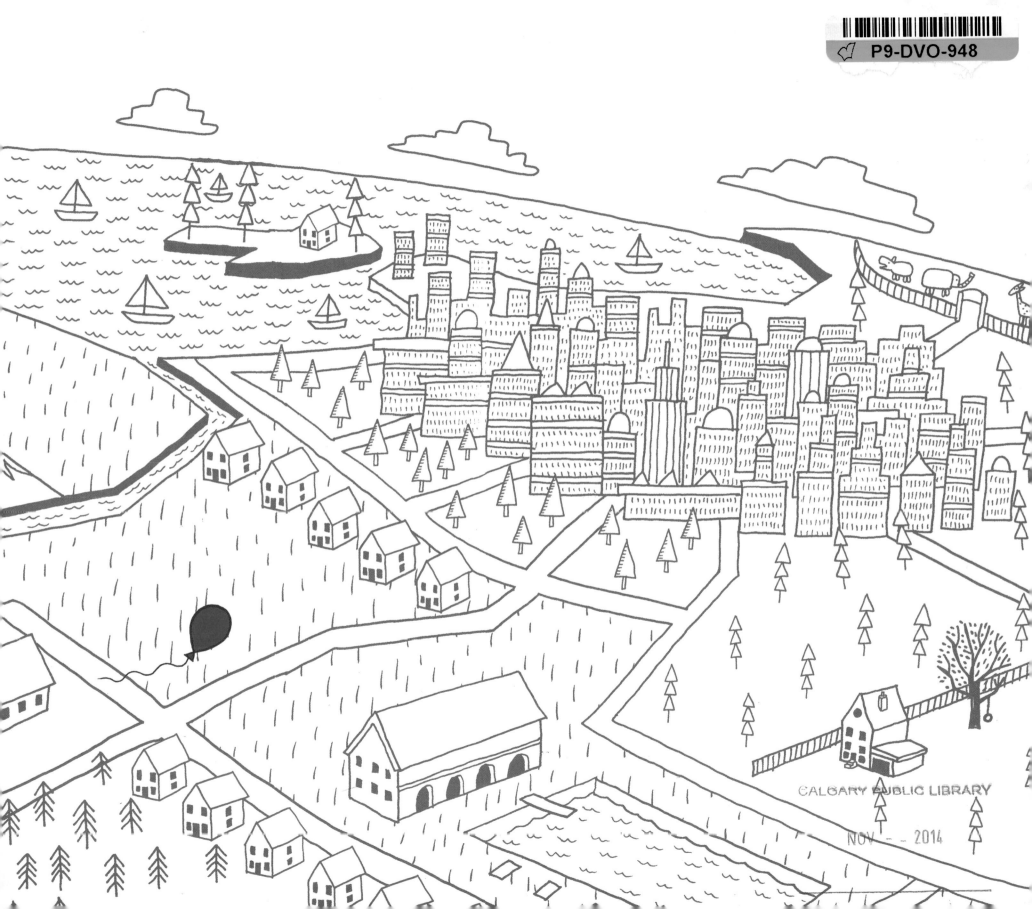

For my reliable test pilots –
Ruadhán, Fionnabhair, Edmund, William,
Thomas, Maeve and David.

Other books by Chris Judge

THE LONELY BEAST

First American edition published in 2014 by Andersen Press USA, an imprint of Andersen Press Ltd.
www.andersenpressusa.com
First published in Great Britain in 2014 by Andersen Press Ltd., 20 Vauxhall Bridge Road, London SW1V 2SA.
Published in Australia by Random House Australia Pty., Level 3, 100 Pacific Highway, North Sydney, NSW 2060.

Copyright © Chris Judge, 2014.

Distributed in the United States and Canada by
Lerner Publishing Group, Inc.
241 First Avenue North
Minneapolis, MN 55401 USA
For reading levels and more information, look up this title at www.lernerbooks.com.

Color separated in Switzerland by Photolitho AG, Zürich.
Printed and bound in Malaysia by Tien Wah Press.

Library of Congress Cataloging-in-Publication data available.
ISBN: 978-1-4677-5013-4
eBook ISBN: 978-1-4677-5016-5
1 – TWP – 1/28/14

TiN

CHRIS JUDGE

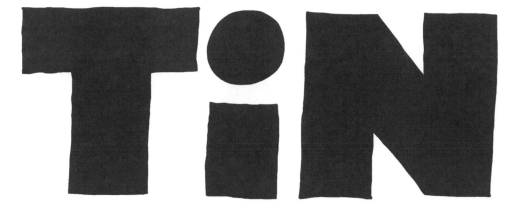

Andersen Press USA

Tin's mom asked him to look after his little sister, Nickel, for the afternoon.

"No problem," said Tin.

"Nickel, you play with your toys while I read my comic," said Tin, relaxing.

But the peace didn't last for long. "What's the matter, Zinc?" asked Tin.

"NICKEL!
How did you get up
there so quickly?"
yelled Tin in horror.

Tin jumped up the tree after Nickel.

Higher and higher they climbed . . .

. . . but just as Tin reached her . . .

She floated away!

Tin scrambled down the tree and jumped on his bicycle.

Tin and Zinc chased Nickel all the way to the big city.

Tin rode as fast as he could.   Round and round, and up and up.

"I've got you Nickel!" exclaimed Tin, bravely leaping into the air.

Tin, Nickel and Zinc slowly drifted up over the city until, unfortunately, the balloon burst.

PoP!

"This is not good," he said.

"Oh dear," cried Tin, as they plummeted down through the air.

"Not good at all . . ."

Luckily, just at that moment . . .

...a big parade was passing beneath them.

Tin and Zinc landed with a BUMP on the back of a large, gray elephant.

While Nickel landed safely on the back of a long-necked giraffe.

But then all of the animals turned and marched into the Safari park!

The elephant went one way . . .

... and the giraffe the other!

Tin and Zinc slid down the elephant's trunk.

But Nickel was too quick for them!

They raced across the shells of three shocked tortoises.

Hurried past a daydreaming lion.

Ran between the legs of a
pink flamingo.

Through the mouth of a
surprised hippo.

Across the back of a strolling rhino.

Up and down a great big snake.

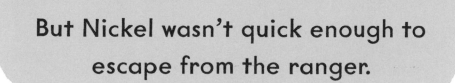

But Nickel wasn't quick enough to escape from the ranger.

"Oh Nickel, you gave us such a fright!" said Tin.

"I'm glad you are okay, but please don't do that again!" he said,
handing her a new balloon.

It was getting dark, so Tin found his bicycle and they all raced home before Mom noticed they were gone.

"Well done, Tin! You deserve a treat for looking after your sister," said his mother, proudly.

"It was easy-peasy," said Tin.

WOOF! WOOF! WOOF!